CHECKING FOR CHUCKS
IN THE
SUMMERTIME

Allon Standifird

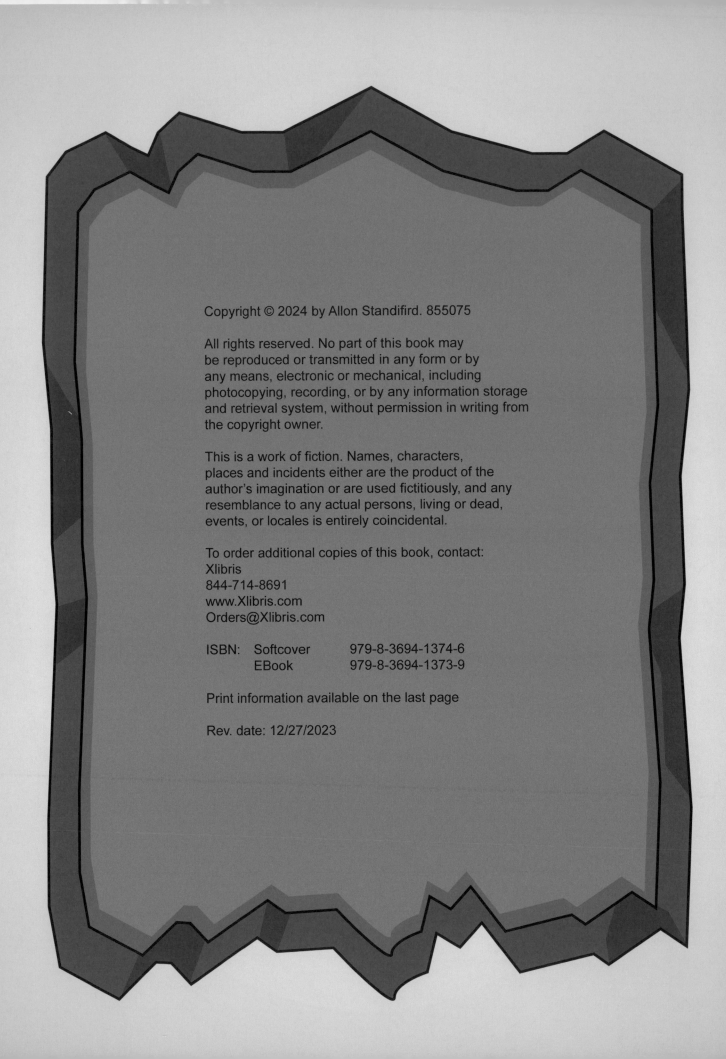

To order additional copies of this book, contact:
Xlibris
844-714-8691
www.Xlibris.com
Orders@Xlibris.com

ISBN: Softcover   979-8-3694-1374-6
        EBook   979-8-3694-1373-9

Print information available on the last page

Rev. date: 12/27/2023

CHECKING FOR CHUCKS IN THE SUMMERTIME

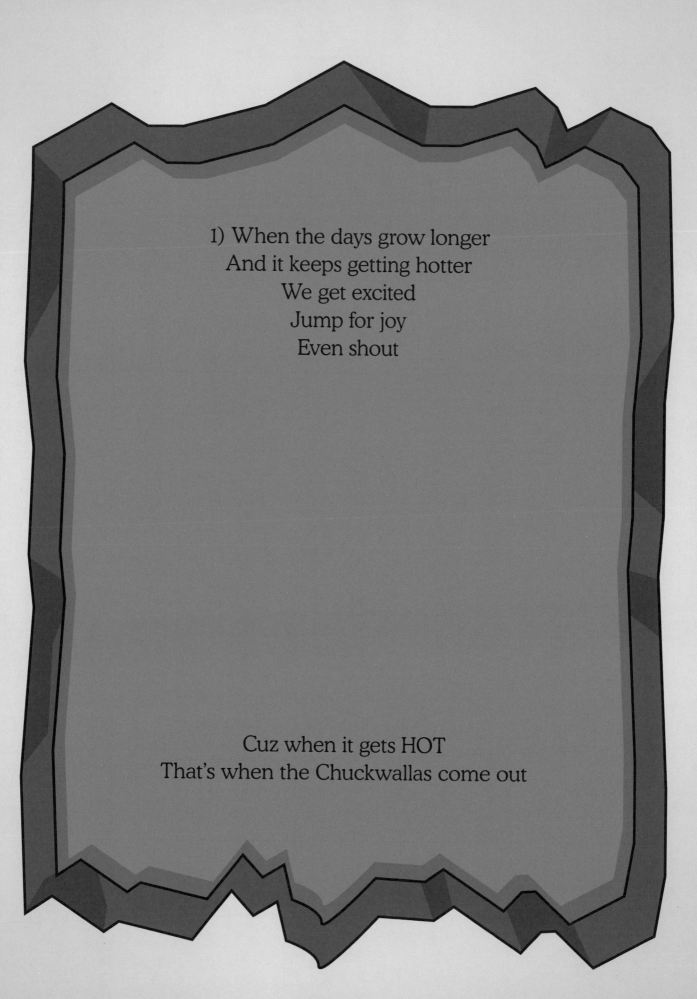

1) When the days grow longer
And it keeps getting hotter
We get excited
Jump for joy
Even shout

Cuz when it gets HOT
That's when the Chuckwallas come out

2) Sitting high on the mountain rocks
Soaking up the Sun
The carrot tail chuckwalla is always looking for danger
And ready to run
So the only way to watch him is
with great patience and charm,
Assuring the lizard we'll not come too close
and certainly mean no harm

AND THIS IS OUR FAVORITE WAY
To be Checking for Chucks

Me and my sister and little brother too,
Jump with Uncle Joe into one of his trucks

Up the mountain we go
And it's hot!
100°, maybe 105
Hot enough to wonder what could
be out and still be alive!
But we are not hot. We are in the tallest of Uncle
Joe's trucks with AC blasting ice cold,
Keeping us cool while checking for Chucks

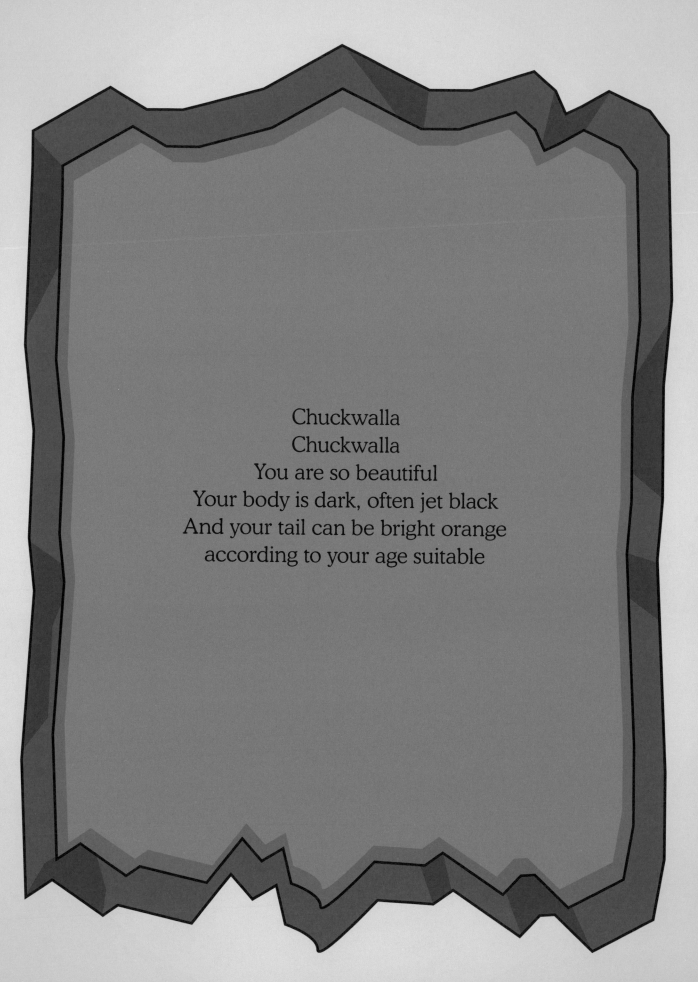

Chuckwalla
Chuckwalla
You are so beautiful
Your body is dark, often jet black
And your tail can be bright orange
according to your age suitable

We sit up high in the tallest of Uncle Joe's trucks
cuz that's the best view of the high sitting Chucks
Uncle Joe goes very very slow
so we can spot them on high
long before we draw nigh

Then Uncle Joe will pull over to let the line
of cars and trucks behind us pass
Then he pulls forward very very slow.
As slow as a little bug we approach the regal chuckwalla

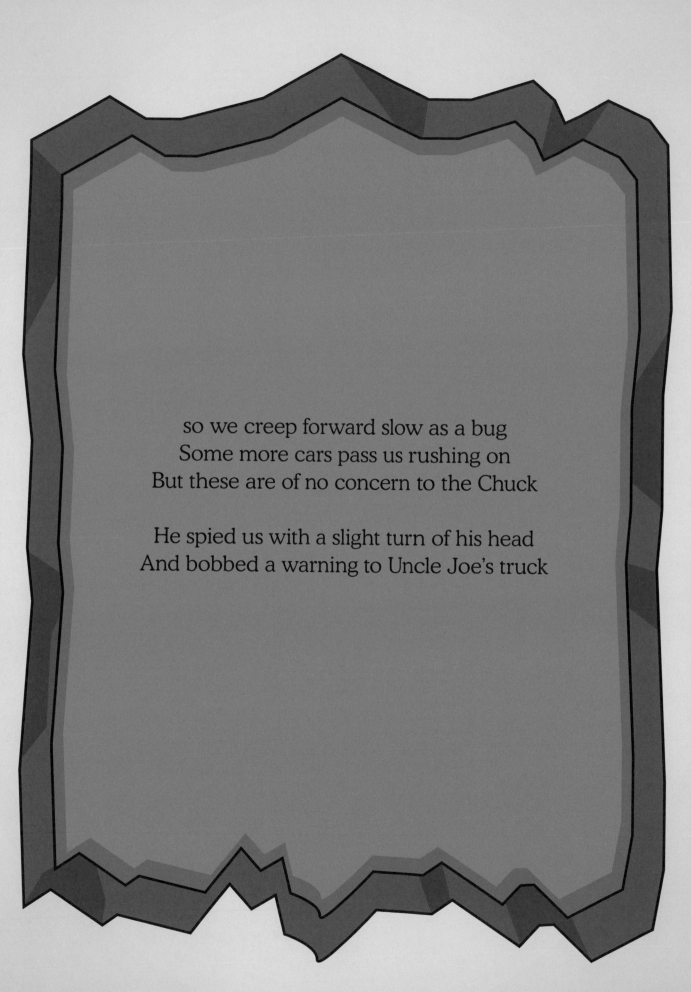

so we creep forward slow as a bug
Some more cars pass us rushing on
But these are of no concern to the Chuck

He spied us with a slight turn of his head
And bobbed a warning to Uncle Joe's truck

"Whisper in quite voices, kids" says Uncle Joe
"And give off GOOD VIBES.
Remember,
Predators will eat a chuckwalla
And they are always afraid for their lives"

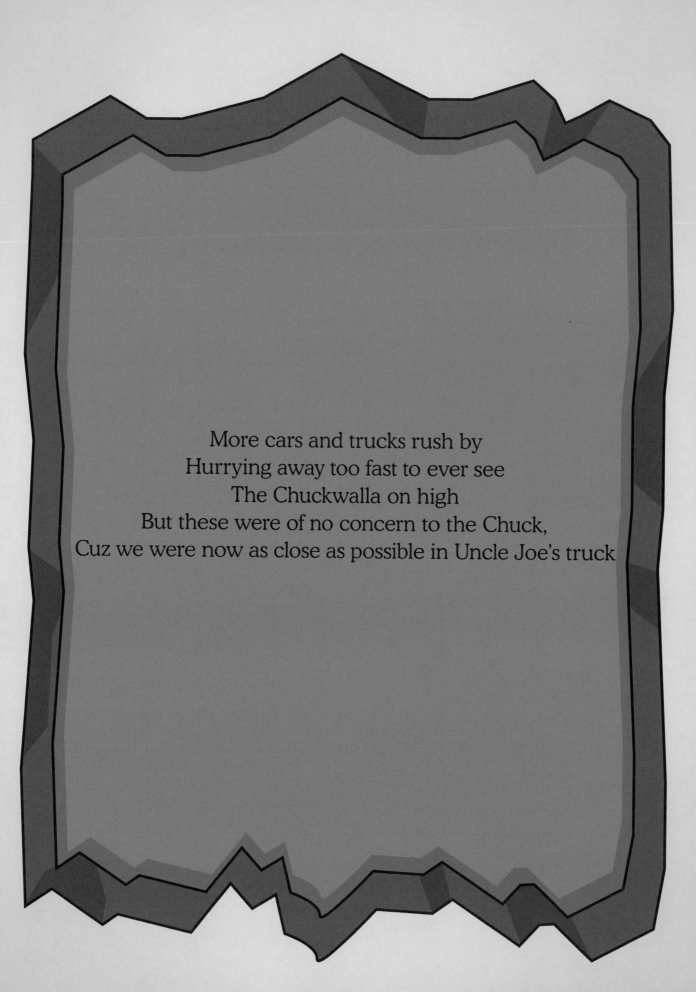

More cars and trucks rush by
Hurrying away too fast to ever see
The Chuckwalla on high
But these were of no concern to the Chuck,
Cuz we were now as close as possible in Uncle Joe's truck

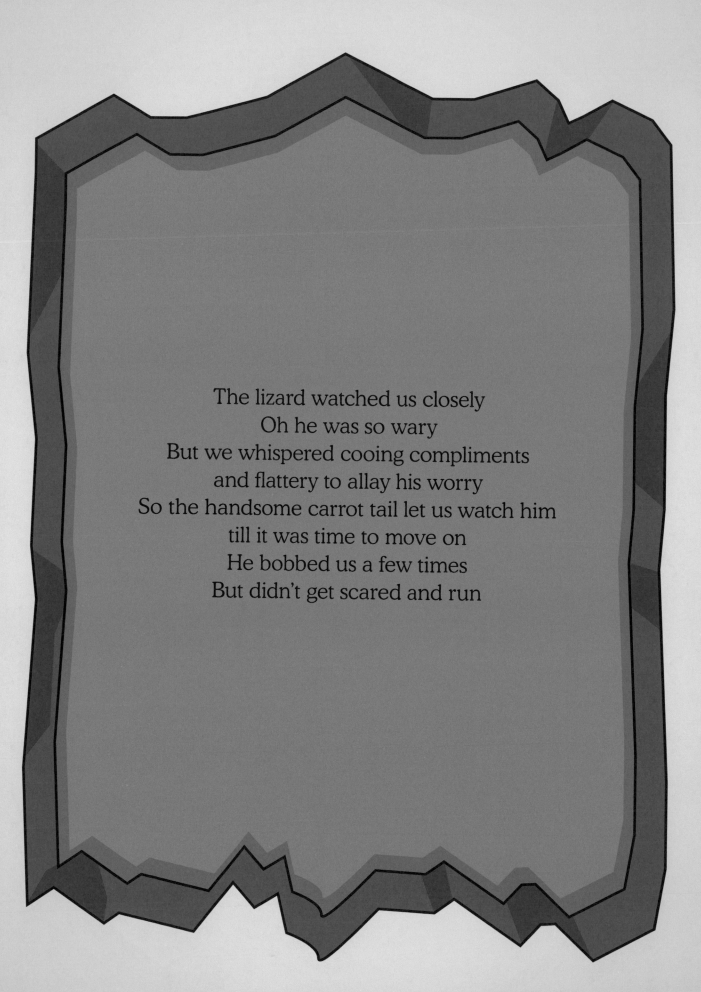

The lizard watched us closely
Oh he was so wary
But we whispered cooing compliments
and flattery to allay his worry
So the handsome carrot tail let us watch him
till it was time to move on
He bobbed us a few times
But didn't get scared and run

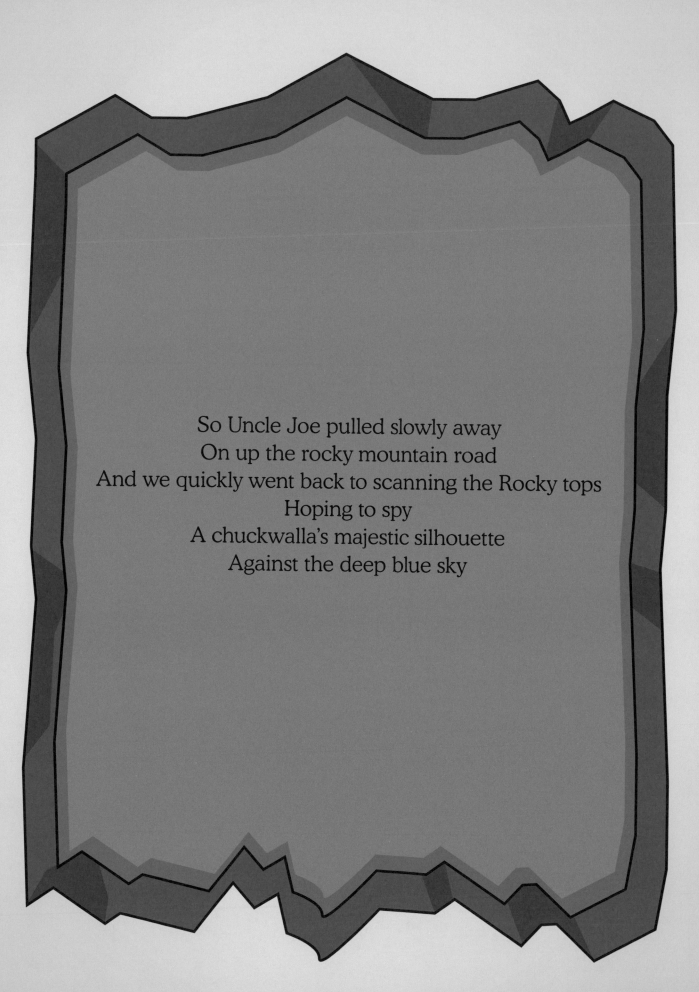

So Uncle Joe pulled slowly away
On up the rocky mountain road
And we quickly went back to scanning the Rocky tops
Hoping to spy
A chuckwalla's majestic silhouette
Against the deep blue sky

Outside it is blazing hot hot hot
But here in the tallest of Uncle Joe's trucks
We're as cool as cucumbers with the AC blasting
Which is our favorite way to be checking for Chucks

CARROT TAIL CHUCKWALLA

Sauromalus ater
Diet: Herbivorous

FEMALE

MALE

Best viewing

Spring and fall: any sunny day above 80°
Summer: Mornings and days up to 102°
Sometimes can be seen above 102°, in the shade of the
brittle bush whose yellow flowers are a favored food

Best viewing in Phoenix Arizona;

South mountain park preserve
White tanks park preserve
Camelback mountain

Printed in the United States
by Baker & Taylor Publisher Services